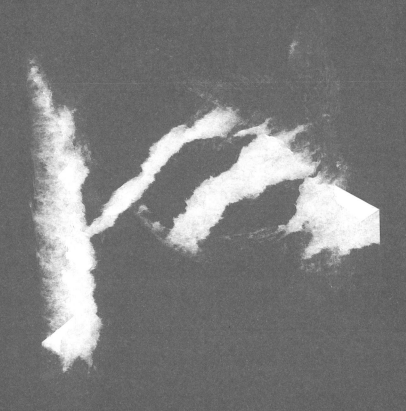

ALADDIN
& HIS MAGICAL LAMP

Retold by Katie Daynes

Illustrated by
Paddy Mounter

Reading Consultant: Alison Kelly
Roehampton University

Contents

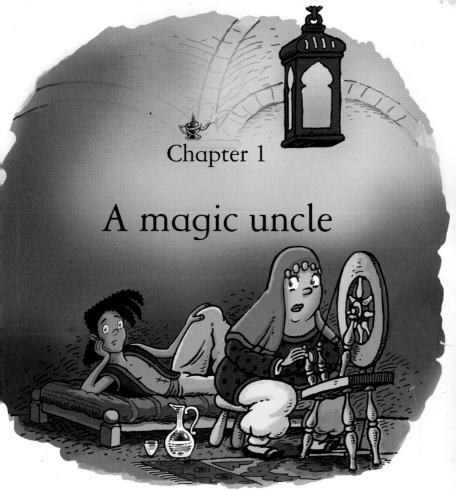

Chapter 1

A magic uncle

There was once a lazy boy named Aladdin. His dad, who had to run the family business alone, died of worry. Aladdin's mother was in despair.

3

One day, Aladdin was messing around as usual when a man came up to him.

"Aladdin!" he cried. "It's me, Uncle Abanazar, your father's long-lost brother!"

I didn't know I had an uncle.

I've been away for many years.

That evening, Aladdin's new uncle invited himself to supper.

When he heard that Aladdin didn't have a job, he bought him a fancy store to run.

Aladdin and his mother were very happy. Neither of them guessed Abanazar was really a wicked magician.

The next day,
Abanazar took
Aladdin on a
long walk out of
the city.

"Here we are," said his uncle
at last. He lit a fire, threw
some powder on it and said
some strange words.

A trap door made of stone appeared in the grass. Aladdin was astonished. His uncle could do magic!

"Under this stone there are many treasures, but I only want one," said Abanazar. "Bring me the lamp."

"Take this ring. It will protect you," he added, pushing Aladdin down the steps. Aladdin went through four rooms of gold, into a garden of fruit trees. The fruit sparkled like pieces of glass.

He saw the lamp, stuffed it into his pocket, then picked handfuls of the pretty fruit.

"Hand me the lamp," cried Abanazar from the entrance.

But Aladdin had taken too long finding it. Abanazar thought he'd been tricked.

How dare you keep the lamp for yourself!

Before Aladdin could answer, there was a loud thud and everything went dark.

Chapter 2

Two genies

Aladdin was trapped. It was cold, dark and very spooky. He rubbed his hands to keep warm.

Suddenly, a huge man rose
up in front of him.

"I am the genie of the ring,"
he boomed.
"What can I
do for you?"

Wow!

"Get me out of here!" shouted
Aladdin. In a flash, he found
himself outside on the grass.

He rushed home to tell his mother what had happened.

"Abanazar can't be my uncle. He did magic things and tried to kill me!" he cried.

"You and your stories," said his mother. "Now, what do you want for supper? I'll sell that old lamp to buy some food."

She started to polish the
lamp and jumped back in
fright as a giant man
floated out.

I am the genie
of the lamp.
Your wish is my
command.

"Do you have any food?"
asked Aladdin. "I'm starving."
In an instant, a huge feast
appeared on silver plates.

13

The food and wine lasted for
a week. When it had gone,
Aladdin sold the silver plates.

Now life was easy. If
Aladdin or his mother wanted
food, Aladdin just rubbed the
lamp and asked the genie.

One day, Aladdin was at the market selling plates when he saw some sparkling jewels.

"They're just like the glass fruit I picked in the cave," he thought in amazement.

It wasn't glass after all!

He ran straight home, found the jewels he'd picked in the cave and hid them.

Chapter 3

The Sultan's daughter

Early one morning, there was
a command from the Sultan.

"Princess Badr-al-Budur will
go to the public baths today.
Everyone must stay at home."

Aladdin wondered what the fuss was about. He hid at the baths so he could see the princess for himself.

When she lifted her veil, Aladdin almost fainted. The only female face he'd seen before was his mother's. But Princess Badr was beautiful!

He skipped home with starry eyes and a silly smile.

"Whatever's the matter?" asked his mother.

"I'm in love with the Sultan's daughter," he sighed.

I must marry her.

His mother laughed but Aladdin was serious.

"If I don't marry Badr, I'll die," he said.

He begged his mother to ask the Sultan for his daughter.

"Take him these jewels as a gift," he added.

"The Sultan will never agree!" cried his mother. But she was very worried about her son, so she did as he asked.

The Sultan lived in a grand palace. On her first visit, the Sultan didn't even look at Aladdin's mother. But she went back again and again until, finally, he spoke to her.

Why do you keep coming to my palace?

She told the Sultan about
her son's love for Princess Badr.
   "We are not worthy of your
greatness," she mumbled. "But
here is a small gift."

I've never
seen jewels
so big!

   "Hmm... Badr does need a
husband..." the Sultan said.
   "But you said *my* son could
marry her," cried the thin man
beside him.

The man was a powerful lord called a vizier. He whispered something in the Sultan's ear, then the Sultan turned to Aladdin's mother.

"Your son can marry my daughter in three months' time," he said.

Chapter 4

The wrong husband

Two months later, Aladdin's mother was in the city. Everyone was talking about a royal wedding.

"Princess to marry vizier's son today!" shouted a herald.

Aladdin's mother rushed
home to tell Aladdin the bad
news. He was very upset, until
he remembered the genie of
the lamp.

He ordered the genie to
disturb the couple that
very night.

Put the vizier's
son out in the cold
and bring Princess
Badr to me.

At midnight, the genie brought Badr to Aladdin's house and left the vizier's son in the dark, damp street.

"You're safe with me," said Aladdin softly.

Before sunrise, the genie returned Badr and the vizier's son to their room.

"What's wrong?" asked Badr's parents at breakfast.

You look awful!

Princess Badr kept very quiet. That evening, the vizier's son prayed for a peaceful night's sleep, but at midnight the genie came again...

After another cold night on the street, the vizier's son had had enough.

"I'm sorry, Sultan," he said. "Your daughter's wonderful but I can't cope with these horrible nightmares."

"Ah well, it wasn't meant to be," replied the Sultan and he ended the marriage.

Chapter 5

Aladdin gets married

Before long, Aladdin's mother went back to see the Sultan.

"Tell your son to send me more jewels," he told her.

"I want forty plates full," he went on, "carried by eighty servants dressed in silk. Only then can Aladdin marry Badr."

The genie managed this easily. Within an hour, a long procession was on its way.

The Sultan couldn't believe
his eyes.

"Tell your son he can marry
my daughter right away!" he
told Aladdin's mother.

But first, Aladdin wanted a home for Badr. He described his perfect palace to the genie and the genie built it overnight.

...marble floors, jewels in the walls...

Aladdin rode to the Sultan's palace dressed in his finest clothes. The wedding day began with music and dancing and finished with feasting and fireworks.

That evening, Badr went to her new home. She was delighted. Aladdin was the most handsome man she'd ever seen and their palace was the best in the world.

Chapter 6

Abanazar returns

Far away in the desert, Abanazar learned of Aladdin's good fortune.

"He must have escaped with the lamp," he snarled.

He went to Aladdin's city to find the lamp. "New lamps for old!" he shouted.

New lamps for old!

Badr heard the shouts from her palace.

"That sounds good," she thought and found an old lamp to give him.

Abanazar ran to a quiet corner and rubbed the lamp.

"What can I do for you?" asked the genie.

"Take me, the palace and the princess to the middle of the desert," said Abanazar.

Later that morning, the Sultan looked from his window and nearly fainted.

"My d-daughter's p-palace has g-gone," he said.

He thought Aladdin had tricked him and sent some soldiers to arrest him.

Aladdin returned from a hunting trip to find a group of soldiers and no palace. He was just as surprised as the Sultan.

"Don't worry, I'll find your daughter," he promised.

You'd better, or else you're dead.

Aladdin clasped his hands together in despair and the genie of the ring appeared.

"Oh! I'd forgotten about you!" said Aladdin. "Please help me."

"I can't bring Badr to you," he replied, "but I can take you to her."

Seconds later, Aladdin was beneath Badr's window.

A wicked man tricked me!

"Don't worry!" Aladdin called. "I have a plan. Agree to eat with him tonight. I'll sneak in with some poison and you can put it in his wine."

40

Abanazar was so busy gazing at Badr, he didn't see her poison his drink. After one sip, he fell to the ground and died.

Aladdin searched the palace for his lamp. One wish later, he and Badr were home.

Chapter 7

The evil brother

But they still weren't safe.
Abanazar had an evil brother
and he wanted revenge.

The brother dressed up as Fatima, a holy woman. He stood outside Aladdin's palace pretending to heal people.

Badr was very excited to see Fatima and invited her inside.

"What a lovely hall," said the fake Fatima. "But if you hang a roc's egg from the dome, it will be even better."

The roc was an enormous bird which laid huge white eggs. Badr loved Fatima's suggestion and asked Aladdin.

"No problem," he said, and called the genie of the lamp.

Bring me a roc's egg.

WHAT?!

"Anything but that!" wailed the genie. "If you ask for such a thing, I must kill you!"

"But I know it wasn't your idea," he went on. "Fatima is really Abanazar's brother in disguise. He wants you dead!"

Aladdin was shocked. He had to think fast.

Oh my head's so sore.

He asked Fatima to heal his headache. As the evil brother came closer, Aladdin grabbed his dagger and killed him.

With no more evil men to bother them, Aladdin and Badr were safe.

In time, Aladdin became Sultan and his mother became a grandmother. They had all they could wish for, so the lamp and ring were left in a drawer. Who knows... the genies may still be there today.

There are lots more great stories for you to read:

Usborne Young Reading: Series One
Animal Legends
Stories of Dragons
Stories of Giants
Stories of Gnomes & Goblins
Stories of Magical Animals
Stories of Pirates
Stories of Princes & Princesses
Stories of Witches
The Burglar's Breakfast
The Dinosaurs Next Door
The Monster Gang
Wizards

Usborne Young Reading: Series Two
A Christmas Carol
Aesop's Fables
Gulliver's Travels
Jason & The Golden Fleece
Robinson Crusoe
The Adventures of King Arthur
The Amazing Adventures of Hercules
The Amazing Adventures of Ulysses
The Clumsy Crocodile
The Fairground Ghost
The Incredible Present
Treasure Island

Aladdin and his magical lamp comes from
a collection of Arabian stories known as *The
Thousand and One Nights*. In early tellings of the
story, the wicked magician isn't named. But in
the first *Aladdin* pantomime he's called Abanazar,
so that's the name we've used here.

Series editor: Lesley Sims

Designed by
Russell Punter

This edition first published in 2007 by Usborne Publishing Ltd.,
Usborne House, 83-85 Saffron Hill, London EC1N 8RT, England.
www.usborne.com Copyright © 2007, 2003 Usborne Publishing Ltd.